THE Christmas CLOCK

Illustrated by Soren Sturlaugson

Time Stops

Hope Prevails

Christmas Awaits

written by Brett Roeper

The Christmas Clock

Copyright ©2023 by Brett Roeper

For Mom, Dad,
Brooke and Addie.

For Emma, Kate and Sevvi

Y a todos mis
amigos de
Colombia que
no van a
entender
porque abren
sus regalos a
medianoche!

"Bye, Merry Christmas!" I yelled from the car as Mom and Dad loaded the presents into the trunk. Snow slowly drifted down from the sky above, setting up a _perfect_ Christmas Eve.

"Get in the car **dork**," my sister's voice broke through the momentary silence. I gave her a shove and climbed in the backseat.

As we rolled on down the highway back to our house in Chagrin Falls, breaking news blared across the radio, "Santa's sleigh has just been spotted streaking across the sky over Toronto, Canada. Stayed tuned for more announcements."

The Christmas music clicked back on. **"DID YOU HEAR THAT!"** I yelled.

"Toronto isn't far! <u>Step on it!</u>"

"Take it easy son." answered Dad. "Santa may not have speed limits, but unfortunately we still do."

My sister stuck her foot in my face, "what do you care anyways? Santa's giving you a BIG LUMP of coal."

I stuck out my tongue and started thinking about **CHRISTMAS MORNING**. The most beautiful sight in the world, a fire in the fireplace, snow covering the ground, and a Christmas tree surrounded by presents. only a few short hours away.

After what seemed like an <u>eternity</u> we finally pulled into the driveway. The car didn't turn off before I was already out the door running past the Christmas TREE.

"Brett, slow down!" my mom shouted from the car. Didn't she understand?? The quicker I can get ready for bed, the faster SANTA can come to the house, and the sooner we are until Christmas morning. If I need to run a little bit to make that happen, so be it.

was already half way done brushing my teeth by the time I heard my sister coming down the stairs. She didn't seem to have any rush. what's the deal with that? "Brooke," I gargled with a mouth full of toothpaste, "huuurrry up, get ready for bed." As I spoke flecks of toothpaste shot out of my mouth like *MISSILES* spraying the mirror. Mom wouldn't like that one bit.

Brooke saw the mess, "I hope for your sake Santa doesn't punish slobs!" I gave the mirror a quick <u>once over</u> with my shirt sleeve. As she walked into her room she casually mentioned, "Yeah, that's going to help. When you're done we can leave out the note and cookies for Santa."

Mom and Dad were in the kitchen doing whatever parents do on Christmas Eve. Me however, I had a <u>mission</u>: cookies, milk, note, prayers, bed, and sleep. What does that all **=** ?

SANTA, and a rockin' Christmas morning.

After Dad read us <u>*Twas the Night Before Christmas*</u> we poured a glass of milk and set out the cookies.

"So Brett, what are you going to write to Santa this year?" Dad asked.

"Well frankly Dad." I answered. "I want to tell him I'm a little concerned about his health. I mean this guy is eating like 4 billion cookies a night. Can you imagine poor Mrs. Claus dealing with that once he gets home later? Toot central. Yikes! I see a night on the couch in Santa's future."

Dad and Mom laughed. I even managed to get a giggle out of my sister. "Next year we'll make sure to leave him some orange slices and some V8 juice." Dad chuckled. "You two better get downstairs for bed."

"This is the ONE night of the year you don't have to tell me twice." I responded. "Sweet dreams. Merry Christmas! See y'all in the morning."

My mom came in my room as I changed into my pajamas, a nice festive affair, green and red stripes. I'm sure the other third graders at Sands Elementary would love to lay their eyes on this scene. I'd never hear the end of it. BUT I'll wear anything I need to wear to get the fatman (and I use this term in the most _endearing_ way) down the chimney.

I was getting anxious, I wanted to get to bed. "MOM, what are you doing?" I whined. She was always touching stuff. Mom's are weird like that. "Sorry dear," she replied, "are you ready for bed?" "Yes," I replied, Then she did

the normal <u>Mom routine</u>:

"Brush your teeth?"

"Yes."

"Wash your face?"

"Yes."

"Floss?"

"Yes." (I lied)

"Say your prayers?"

"Yes."

"Alright then, climb into bed."

I jumped into bed. She came over, kissed me on the forehead and wished me a Merry Christmas. As she left she turned off my lamp. And there it **GLARED**, my old digital alarm clock with the big red numbers; my Christmas Eve <u>arch nemesis.</u> It read:

11:39

Now up until this point in the story I have neglected to tell you one very important thing. I can NEVER sleep on Christmas Eve!

Anyone else have this problem? I imagine so. Anyways, the time is

Hold on, a second is a second is a second, right? And a minute is a minute, and hour an hour, and so on and so on. You get it. BUT **WHY**, ON Christmas Eve **IS A SECOND A MINUTE, A MINUTE AN HOUR AND AN HOUR NEVER SEEMS TO END???** Can someone please explain this to me? No worries, this year I am going to bed, NO problems. Eyes shut, dreams cued up, Christmas morning in <u>all its glory</u> comes quickly.

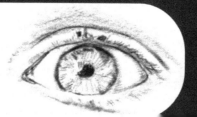

Here we go, closing the eyes, going to sleep.....

okay Brett, you're doing well.

Sleep

Coming

Soon

No problem.

Maybe I'll just peak at the clock. It's probably been 30 or 40 minutes. I know not A LOT of time has passed, but surely close to an hour. Here we go...

11:49! what?! Huh?! 8 minutes, 8 lousy minutes. Calm down Brett, just relax, think of a plan.

YES! Counting sheep, of course. That's a thing right?

I know I have seen that in books and movies.

Alright, a few deep breaths, visualize the sheep,

NO!! Not that **SHEEP**!

That's some kind of llama sheep **MONSTROSITY!**

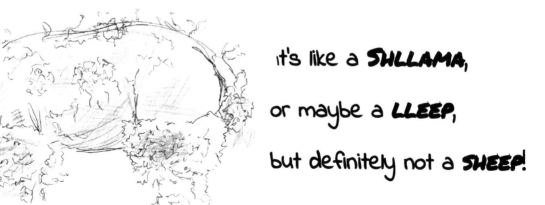

it's like a **SHLLAMA,**

or maybe a **LLEEP,**

but definitely not a **SHEEP!**

Ahhh, yes, there we go, much better.

Wait a minute!

My sheep are just standing around.

Let's get a fence in there.

BETTER

Now to make my sheep jump over the fence. 1 sheep, 2 sheep, 3 sheep, 4 sheep, 5 sheep, 6 sheep, 7 sheep...

HOW PEACEFUL, this is going to work. I can feel myself getting tired already.

8 sheep, 9, sheep...

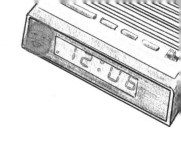

...98 sheep, 99 sheep, 100 sheep, 101 sheep, 102 sheep...

HOW MANY SHEEP DO I HAVE TO COUNT BEFORE I FALL ASHLEEP?! AHHH!

I GIVE UP! **NO MORE SHEEP!**

There aren't enough sheep in the world to make me fall asleep. <u>who</u> came up with that idea anyways?

HORRIBLE, JUST HORRIBLE.

Bretty-Boy, Brettttt, **RELAX**, you're still good baby. Just get a new plan. Everyone says you have a good work ethic, you never give up, (I guess I did give up on that sheep idea pretty quickly though), not important, **FOCUS!** okay, here we go, new rule. No opening your eyes until morning.

NO MATTER WHAT!

If I keep my eyes closed I'll have to fall asleep eventually. That's it, that's the new plan. No matter what happens you just keep your eyes closed.

What a plan, YOU DA' MAN Brett, nothing can stop you now. I'm sure the hours are flying by.

Santa

   would

      be

   impressed!

Wow, hours must have passed by now. I know that I technically haven't **"SLEPT"** yet, but your eyes have been closed **FOREVER!**

Christmas morning will be here before you know it.

MAAAAAAAAN, I WANT TO OPEN MY EYES!

Not yet Bretty, not yet! You're doing great. Think of how rewarding it will be if you can keep your eyes closed for another hour or so, it'll basically be morning by then.

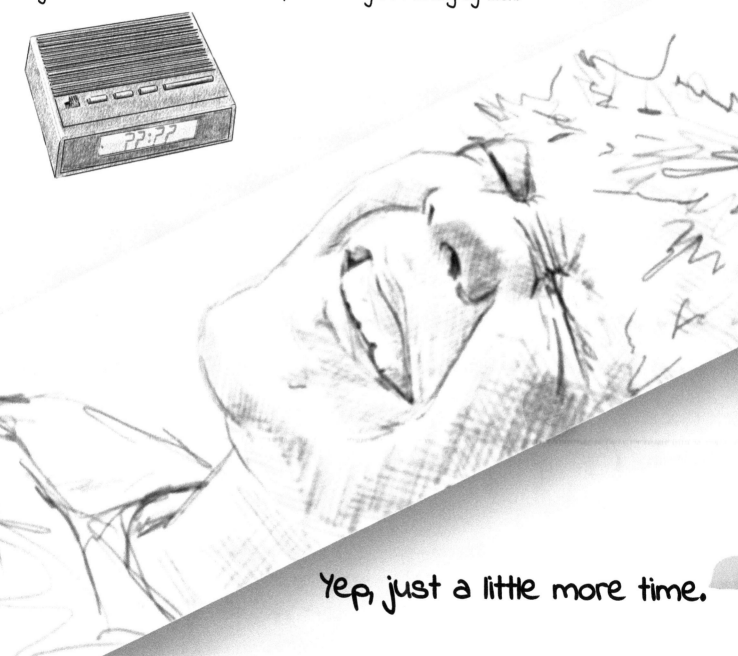

Yep, just a little more time.

KEEP 'EM CLOSED, KEEP 'EM CLOSED!

Ahhh, this is agonizing, maybe just a peak at the clock. Think of how rewarding that will be, and motivating too. It will show you how if you put your mind to something you can do anything.

okay, just a quick peak, a blink of an eye really.

HERE WE GO...

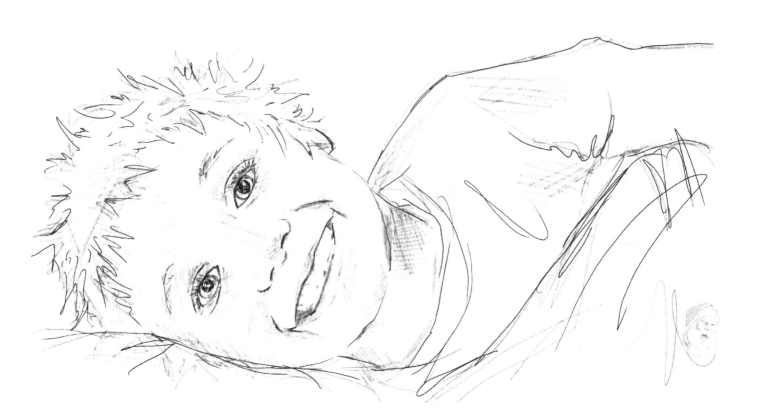

WHAAAAAAAAAAAAAAAAAAAAA!!!!!!

How?!?!?!?

No, no, no, no, **NOOOOOO!**

That's <u>impossible</u>,

18 MINUTES?!??!!?..:...:

UGHHHHHHH!

I'm <u>losing it</u> here!

YOU'RE BLOWING IT!

Kids all over the world will be opening presents tomorrow and you'll be stuck calling 1.800.NorthPole, begging Santa to come back because you **CAN'T** fall asleep.

Think, think, think...

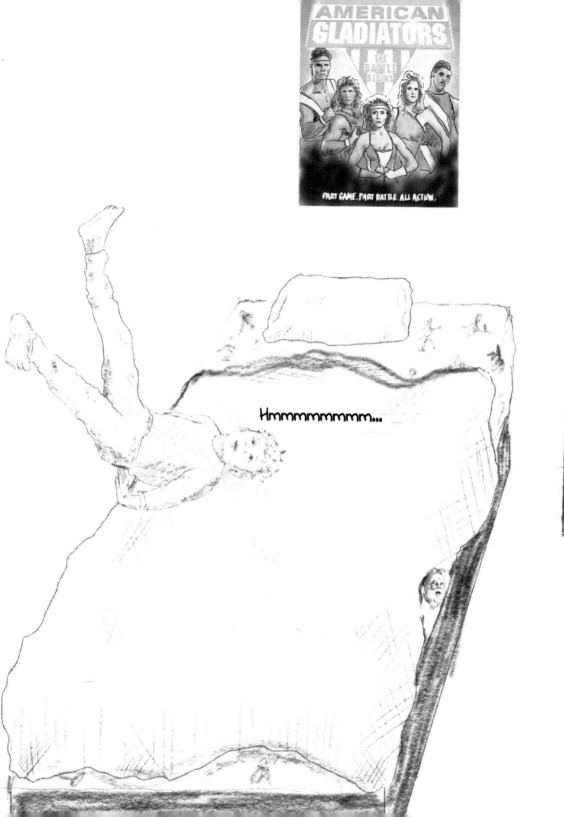

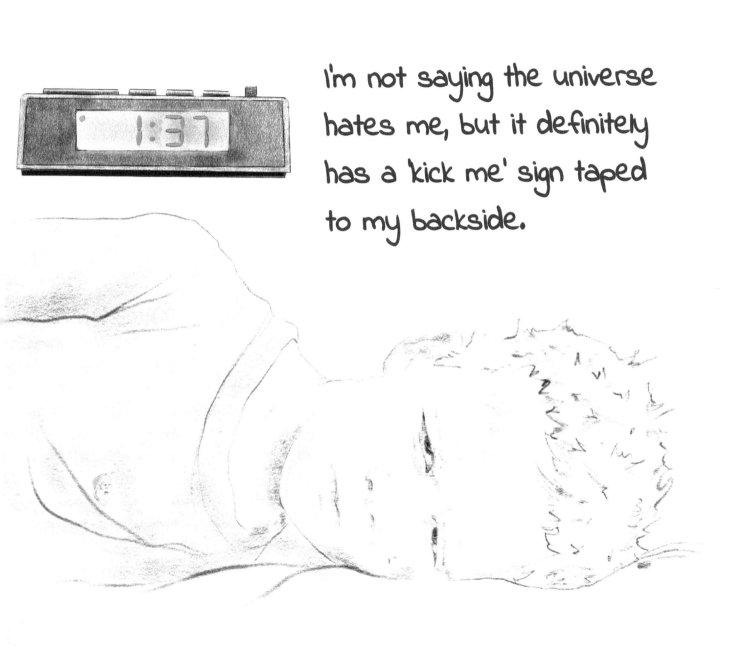

I'm not saying the universe hates me, but it definitely has a 'kick me' sign taped to my backside.